Dear Reader,

Entering the evil world of *Do You Believe?* is difficult for me. I'm one of those people who views the cup as half full, who believes tomorrow offers a chance to start over, and that people are basically good. But open any newspaper, turn on any news program, and you're inundated with mankind's inhumanity. The idea that evil can be subtly woven through the lives of ordinary people, changing their behavior, rotting their psyche, fascinates—and terrifies—me.

It fascinates my hero as well. Writing horror novels has immersed Vic Drummond in the dark side of human nature. Has it made him evil? Or driven him crazy?

Horror has no place in the world of my heroine. Rose Early earns her living photographing happy family groups. She views her world through a camera lens, and with the computer, can "fix" what she doesn't like. Once she meets Vic Drummond, she learns some things can't be fixed.

I chose the Cotswolds in England as the setting for *Do You Believe?* because I can't think of a more picturesque and unlikely place for evil to plant its seeds.

But *Do You Believe?* is not simply the tale of Vic and Rose's encounter with evil. It's also a novel about believing in one's self and most importantly—believing in love.

So . . . ask yourself . . . *Do You Believe?*

Ann Lawrence

Do You Believe?

Ann Lawrence

tor romance

A TOM DOHERTY ASSOCIATES BOOK
NEW YORK

This is a work of fiction. All the characters and events portrayed in this book are either products of the author's imagination or are used fictitiously.

DO YOU BELIEVE?

Copyright © 2005 by Ann Lawrence

Edited by Anna Genoese

A Tor Book
Published by Tom Doherty Associates, LLC
175 Fifth Avenue
New York, NY 10010

www.tor.com

Tor® is a registered trademark of Tom Doherty Associates, LLC.

ISBN 0-765-34888-8
EAN 975-0765-34888-3

First edition: May 2005

Printed in the United States of America

0 9 8 7 6 5 4 3 2 1

Acknowledgments

A book never makes it to publication without the help of many individuals. I'd like to thank the wonderful people who kept me on track throughout the writing of this book.

First, I especially want to thank Martin Roddy, MBE of the Goucestershire Constabulary, England, for his kindness and patience while answering my many questions on police matters as well as numerous other esoteric subjects.

Peter Yonger helped me navigate the world of the Anglican Church. I've taken some ecclesiastic liberties in my book, but none I hope will make a vicar scream. There is no Cotswolds Diocese (or Marleton Village, for that matter).

Ken Kauffman (*www.kenkauffman.com*) gently guided me through the digital photography world.

Christopher Ciavarelli of Ciavarelli Family Funeral Homes explained the ins and outs associated with a family member dying in a foreign country.

My critique partners deserve a medal, especially Sally

Stotter and Lena Pinto, for their patience while reading the many incarnations of this book.

I'm also grateful to my cousin, Kevin Richardson, who helped me keep my British, British.

Last, but never least, I must thank my husband and children who always pick up the slack when the deadline looms. I don't know what I'd do without them!

Any mistakes, whether police procedural, ecclesiastic, photographic, or in British expression are mine and are not to be attributed to any of the marvelous people who helped me during the writing of *Do You Believe?*

"The virtue of the camera is not the power it has to transform the photographer into an artist, but the impulse it gives him to keep on looking."

—Brooks Atkinson, *Once Around the Sun*

1

ROSE EARLY CONSIDERED THE camera angle needed to capture the essence of the English country lane. She thought about the shadows beneath the eaves and how to enhance the vivid colors of the flowers against the warm honey tones of the stone walls.

She'd need to compensate for the dazzle of the sun on the stream that wound along only a few feet from the brightly painted doors. Too bad her camera was back at the bed-and-breakfast.

The door she wanted was a bright, glossy blue. Roses arched over it in a froth of white. To get to the door, she'd have to cross a plank bridge no more than five feet wide.

How hard could that be? Cross a bridge and knock on a door?

She took a deep breath and forced herself to walk casually over the bridge to the door that looked as if it might open onto a stage set in a BBC drama. She reached for the door knocker, but then slowly withdrew her hand.

The gleaming brass knocker was shaped like a gargoyle. The loop of metal that formed the knocker was the gargoyle's finger, crooked to pick its nose.

So, V. F. Drummond had a sense of humor.

Rose knocked. The dull thuds of the heavy brass knocker intruded on the country silence.

After several tries, she looked over at her rented Rover and thought of climbing into it and heading back to Heathrow and home to Pennsylvania. The book under her arm kept her in place.

A man laughed—close by. She followed a stone path to the side of the cottage and peeked into the back garden. It was bordered with picture-postcard English flower beds. In the midst of the waves of lush color stood small topiary animals.

A tall man of about forty, wearing faded jeans and a grimy Rod Stewart T-shirt, clipped at the ears of a boxwood rabbit. Another man, blond and younger by about five years, laughed again. He was not as tall as the gardener, but had a football player—make that rugby player—look about him despite his crisp white shirt and tie.

"Hello," Rose called.

The men swung in her direction. The grubby one frowned, his shears pointed at her like a weapon. "Yeah?"

"I'm looking for V. F. Drummond," she said. Her voice came out high and squeaky. She offered the book.

"Yeah?" He took a step closer, his eyes on the book. He needed a shave. His brown hair looked more in need of a trimming than any of the garden creatures. His manner bordered on hostile.

"Yes. I mean, are you Mr. Drummond?"

"I'm the gardener." He gestured to the rabbit, his tone now frosted with sarcasm.

He looked far too rough to have created the Beatrix Potter world.

"Drummond's not in," he said and turned his back.

"When do you expect him?" She directed her question to the man in the shirt and tie who shrugged.

"Leave your name," the gardener said. He made a decisive, and ruinous, snip to the rabbit's nose.

"Oh. Yes. Here's my card." She fumbled in the pocket of her jacket and withdrew an ivory business card.

Although she extended it to the more civilized man, the gardener plucked it from her fingers.

"What do you want with Drummond?" he asked, shoving the card into the pocket of his jeans.

Rose imagined her card would remain there to be washed illegible at some future time. She dropped the book. As she picked it up, it fell open to the final page.

"I wanted to ask Mr. Drummond a question."

"What question?" Shirt-and-Tie asked.

She shifted her gaze from the book to him. He had an interesting crook to his nose. Maybe he'd been tromped in a rugby scrum. She thought he would not photograph well, whereas the gardener, with his angular cheekbones, dark hair and frown, would make an interesting subject just as he was, dirty T-shirt and all, surrounded by hedge-work animals.

But a photograph was not what she'd come for. Gently, she closed the book and took a deep breath. "Ask Mr. Drummond if he believes in evil."

She turned her back and walked along the stone path, across the miniature bridge to her rental car. As she drove away, reminding herself to keep left, she glanced in her rearview mirror. The two men stood at the side of the cottage, staring after her.

"WHAT WAS THAT ABOUT?" Trevor Harrison asked as he opened a bottle of mineral water.

"I don't know." Vic Drummond said, accepting the bottle. He hooked a chair out from the wrought-iron garden table and slumped into it. He plucked the business card from his pocket.

It read: *Early Photography, Family Portraits for Over Fifty Years*, along with the woman's contact information.

"She's from bloody Pennsylvania, of all places," Vic said.

"Just what's needed, another Yank." Trevor launched into a familiar monologue on American tourists who made life in quiet Marleton Village more pain than pleasure for several months of each year.

"This might change your mind," Vic said. "She's from the Early Photography Studio."

"Early Photography?" Trevor looked over Vic's shoulder at the card. "Then I take it all back; I love Americans." He opened another bottle of water. "Why'd you tell her you were the gardener?"

Vic read the woman's information again. "I'm tired of people coming over here as if I'm some tourist attraction."

"But if she's Joan Early's sister—"

"I don't care if she's the archbishop's mistress. I came here for peace and quiet. I need a drawbridge."

But he smiled as he slid the card into his back pocket.

Rose Early. A man would be happy to rise early for such a pretty woman. Trev was right. He shouldn't have sent her off so soon.

"How's the new book coming?" Trevor asked.

Vic clicked back into the here and now. "Why do you care? You didn't read the last one. In fact, do you read?"

"We coppers haven't the time, what with all the *real* crime about. So tell me what I'm missing, condensed version, of course."

"The new premise is the same as the last," Vic said. "Objects owned by evil people become imbued with their evil—"

"That's a load of rubbish," Trevor interrupted, grinning.

Vic grinned back. "And those objects can pass the evil on to the next owner just as—"

"More rubbish. I'm picturing a car driving around on its own killing people or an umbrella stabbing—"

"Stop interrupting. And the car bit's been done. Aren't miracles and goodness attributed to objects owned by the holy? France is rotten with shrines."

Trevor made a snorting noise.

"I've a serial killer in the last book who gives his ring to a priest just before execution. The moment the priest puts on the ring, he begins to go through life-altering events, ultimately becoming as evil as the killer."

"Perish the thought." Trevor finished off his mineral water. "I'm glad I don't have your imagination. It'd keep me awake at night."

"I'm awake already."

"Where's the new book heading?"

"I'm passing the killer's ring onto another victim."

"You could pass that ring around a long time, but I suppose that's the point."

Vic saluted his friend with his bottle. "At least until the public bores."

Trevor stood up. "I better head back to Stratford. I'm assigned this religious symposium on youth crime, you know. Real work, it is."

"I suppose someone has to protect the holy from having their pockets picked. Sounds tame." Vic hauled himself to his feet as well.

"No religious event is tame since the Iraqi conflict. And with a royal expected, we're overrun with senior police officers and press. At least I'm safe from evil amidst all that holiness."

"Maybe. My Aunt Alice would have argued that."

"I'll miss Alice."

Vic looked over the burgeoning rows of flowers. His Aunt Alice had taken great pride in her garden and it had been in the garden they'd found her, struck down by heart attack.

Sixty-one. Too young to die.

Vic opened and closed the secateurs, inspected a spot of rust. It was hard to accept that his aunt was gone. She had viewed his success with wry amusement. And been one of his toughest critics.

Vic walked Trevor down the garden to the back gate. They shook hands.

"Get over to Stratford for a bit if you can," Trevor said.

"Not if the press is about. I'm allergic to publicity."

Vic watched Trevor walk along a public footpath that ran behind the row of cottages and up to Marleton Village proper.

When Trevor disappeared from view, Vic headed into the cottage. His laptop sat on his Aunt Alice's desk in the sitting room. He turned Rose Early's card over and read it again.

Early Photography. King of Prussia, Pennsylvania.

A place far from Marleton, yet she'd come to see him and ask him the one question he was uncomfortable answering.

He set up a new e-mail message and typed in Rose Early's address. The blank screen with its blinking cursor teased him. His fingers suddenly felt stiff and cold.

He typed one word, hit send, and snapped the laptop closed.

2

Mrs. Bennett hummed around a mouthful of pins. She knelt by the hem of Mrs. Edgar's mother-of-the-bride gown and tucked the blue silk up an inch, slotting pins in with forty-plus years of experience, not really looking or thinking about it.

Mrs. Edgar took a deep breath. "And then I said no smoked oysters. They're too dear."

"Please stand still," Mrs. Bennett said.

"There goes that lovely Vic Drummond." Mrs. Edgar rose on tiptoe to better see the street outside. "You'd never know he was famous, that one. Always has a smile and nod. Took my bag clear up to my door, he did, the other day."

"Did he?" Mrs. Bennett struggled up from her knees and leaned forward to peer out of the bow window of Stitches. Drummond headed into the Pig and Pie.

"Am I finished here?" Mrs. Edgar asked.

"Oh. Yes, luv. Take it off and hang it over the door, will you? There's other work to be done."

While Mrs. Edgar struggled out of her dress and the heavy undergarment she needed to quell the jiggle of flesh gained from years of serving cream teas to the tourist trade of Marleton, Mrs. Bennett wheeled her bicycle out of the shed behind Stitches.

She pedaled toward the looming tower of All Saints Church, Alice Drummond's lovely nephew on her mind.

ROSE DROVE CAUTIOUSLY ALONG the main street of Marleton Village, looking for the lane that led to her bed-and-breakfast.

Marleton, in the Cotswolds, close to Stratford-Upon-Avon, enjoyed more than its share of tourists. It boasted thirteen pubs, one bona fide tea shop, a Norman church, and more quaint cottages and shops than she could shake a stick at.

Why hadn't she asked the men at V. F. Drummond's about her sister Joan?

Because they intimidated you.

Rose reached the village center with its war memorial. She almost circled the obelisk to return and ask the men if they knew Joan, but once in the flow of tourist traffic, she continued straight.

Rose scanned the tourists who wandered past shops and pubs.

Where the heck was Joan?

Rose found her lane, turned into a crushed-stone drive hemmed in with high hedges that within a few yards widened to a courtyard. Cottages bordered the expanse on one side, a lush orchard of pear trees the other.

She parked in front of the first cottage.

"There's irony here, too, somewhere," she said as she ducked past a wooden sign much in need of fresh paint, decorated with entwined roses and thistles.

She hoisted her backpack over one shoulder and knocked on a door marked "Office."

The Rose and Thistle Bed-and-Breakfast was not what she'd expected when she'd arrived that morning. The brochure her sister Joan had left at home pictured a rambling stone "manor house" that could sleep eleven or twelve guests and spoke of cottages—not pictured—that could each sleep two to four.

The cottages proved to be a disappointment. Rose had pictured quaint buildings, like the one in which V. F. Drummond lived—or stayed—according to the man behind the bar at the King's Head Pub. V. F. Drummond, horror novelist, the bartender said, lived in London but had been *staying* in Marleton at his auntie's house until such time as he sold it.

It was expected V. F. Drummond would sell the cottage. Such as *he* were usually found in London, the bartender had whispered, leaning across the bar and glancing left and right before he breathed his words into Rose's ear as if they were some important state secret. London was where *his* kind was usually found.

Came for his auntie's funeral as he should, though. And stayed he had. Been seven weeks now. Letting the roses get a bit leggy, he was, but otherwise didn't cause any trouble.

Rose figured V. F. Drummond just needed to give his gardener a kick in the ass, is all. She wondered about the man who could be comfortable with a Beatrix Potter garden and a horror novel imagination.

Joan's accommodations at the Rose and Thistle were neither quaint nor a cottage, but the end section of what was once a stable block. It had been the calving shed, an idea that didn't bear too much examination.

Something Rose could not avoid examining was why Joan had suddenly stopped answering e-mail or why she had unaccountably packed up and left the bed-and-breakfast when she'd paid for the entire month of July.

Rose knocked again. The proprietor of the Rose and Thistle, Harry Watkins, jerked the door open and frowned at her. Blond and paunchy, Harry looked like the aging coach of Shirt-and-Tie's rugby team.

"More questions?" he asked.

"Have you remembered anything else?"

"Since this morning? No. I told you, your sister left. Saw her drive off, I said." He started to close the door.

"Wait. Please, Mr. Watkins. This is important. And you thought she was skipping out on the bill—"

"Spot on. If she hadn't left her check on the table, you wouldn't be staying in her cottage, mind you." He scratched his paunch and glanced behind him toward the sound of a television.

"She left nothing in the cottage? No clothes?"

"Are you suggesting something, miss?" Suddenly, Watkins looked less impatient and more belligerent.

"No, of course not, I'm just trying to find out what happened to her."

The smile that flickered across his face, and just as quickly disappeared, made Rose's skin crawl.

"Woman looks like her?" he said. "Probably gone to London. None of her sort around here."

Rose bit her tongue on a question about what sort Mr. Watkins imagined Joan to be.

"Is there some place I can check my e-mail?"

He tipped his head. There was a sheen of sweat on his flushed pink skin. "No. Don't think so."

"Do you have a computer? I thought my sister found out about the Rose and Thistle through the Internet."

"We're not on the web. Don't have a computer. Don't see the need. Keep everything up here." He tapped his skull.

Rose forced herself to thank him and headed for Joan's cottage, crossing a lawn studded with daisies no larger than a dime. Beside each door of the stable block "cottages" stood a planter stuffed with pink impatiens, trailing ivy, and scarlet geraniums. Hers had sprouted a pint of milk, the one Mr. Watkins claimed would be delivered daily for her tea.

Tea. She shuddered.

She unlocked the door and entered the cottage for the second time that day. Nothing had changed. No Joan reading on the couch in the tiny living room, or making lunch in the dining-cum-kitchen area. The small bedroom tucked under the eaves still looked bare and unoccupied, white bed linens folded at the foot of the bed.

The possibility of Joan popping in soon dimmed when

Rose placed the pint of milk on the bare shelves of the refrigerator. Or did her sister eat every meal in a restaurant?

Certainly, there was no breakfast at the Rose and Thistle for cottage occupants. The breakfast part of the bed-and-breakfast applied only to the manor house guests.

Rose dropped her backpack on the floor between the two single beds in the downstairs bedroom and unpacked her luggage, a small carry-on suitcase. But when she placed her toothpaste and birth control pills in the medicine cabinet of the bathroom, they looked so forlorn on the shelf, as lonely as the milk in the empty refrigerator, she grabbed them and tucked them away in her backpack.

The feeling of emptiness did not dissipate as she opened a cardboard carton—something missed by Harry Watkins and found by her in the back of a cupboard filled with brooms and buckets.

The box was Rose's only evidence that Joan had ever occupied the cottage. Acid surged into Rose's throat. Why had Joan gone off without word to anyone?

Feeling like a voyeur into her sister's life, Rose dug in the box, strewing the contents across the white duvet.

The carton contained folders, scraps of paper, and a jumble of pamphlets and brochures about English churches. She perched on the spare bed and examined the folders. The first held neatly typed notes for Joan's current project, a book on religious art, commissioned by the Cotswolds Diocese of the Church of England.

Photographic essays on esoteric subjects were Joan's specialty. Coffee table books for snobby intellectuals, Rose preferred to call them.

The second folder held receipts. Unlike the typed notes, the receipts were crumpled, stained, or showed some other evidence of having been carelessly stuffed into a pocket or purse.

Rose read one, a receipt from Edgar's Tea Shop. Her throat felt thick picturing Joan lavishing jam on scones. According to her e-mail messages, Joan had gained ten pounds since coming to England three months before.

Rose smoothed each receipt and sorted them by date before tucking them away.

Dozens of photographs of altar screens, statuary, choir stalls, and gargoyles filled the last folder. The earliest of the photographs was dated 1970, the latest, this year. Those were Joan's work.

Joan's photography was in the form of contact sheets. Each sheet was filled with thirty-six tiny snapshots, an easy way to look over images before choosing those that would appear in the book.

Joan disdained the digital camera, preferring to shoot dozens of rolls of film and accepting a certain amount of waste.

Even as small images on the contact sheets, Joan's photographs showed they were not just an attempt to capture religious subjects for reference purposes. The pictures were works of art in light and shadow, color and form. A celebration of religious fervor.

Several altar screens had been photographed a score of times at various times of day, in artificial light and candle glow. The book promised to be visually spectacular.

If Joan finished it.

The contact sheets were clipped to a database. Each photograph was neatly catalogued by a reference number, a date, and the church in which the particular piece was found. Some entries had additional notes on the artist who'd made the piece. Two altar screens, Rose read, dated back to the thirteenth century.

Rose skimmed copies of church documents. They were the start of what Rose knew would be a sizeable collection of information needed by Joan to write the book's text.

Rose set the folders aside. She picked up a heavy black object, a wide-angle camera lens.

"Where are you, Joan?" Rose asked, rubbing her thumb over the JE etched on the side of the lens.

She wrapped the lens in a T-shirt. Before she stuffed it into her camera backpack, she took out the book that had been on the bottom of the carton.

Do You Believe in Evil? by V. F. Drummond.

Joan was as contemptuous of commercial fiction as she was of digital photography. If she read at all, it was something Rose would call depressing and Joan mind-expanding.

V. F. Drummond was Great Britain's answer to Stephen King. His book was as unlikely a read for Joan as a romance. Joan didn't believe in happy endings any more than she believed in ghosts and ghoulies.

Joan's notes filled the margins throughout Drummond's book. She'd marked passages with a yellow highlighter.

But it was the note on the last page that had scared Rose and sent her to the cottage with the blue door.

Joan had written, "I believe."

3

THE PIG AND PIE, one of Marleton's thirteen pubs, sported doves copulating on its cupola and a peacock screaming at cars in the parking lot. The inside was less exotic, wood-paneled, utilitarian. Rose was determined to ask about her sister in every one of them if necessary. She kicked herself again for not asking V. F. Drummond's gardener and his companion about Joan. Maybe it had just been jet lag that left her tongue-tied.

Rose took a seat in front of a dusty window whose tiny panes looked like they were cut from the bottom of a bottle. She studied the blackboard offerings for a few moments before going to the bar to place an order for steak and kidney pie and a pint of the local ale.

She saw V. F. Drummond's gardener when she returned to her seat, playing darts in a corner with several men. He wore a cleaner T-shirt—Sting, this time—but the jeans were the same faded ones from the afternoon. At least he hadn't washed her card yet.

He wore grass-stained sneakers, or trainers as Joan had called them soon after her arrival. The use of the British terms in place of American ones was just another example of Joan showing off.

Joan had worked the terms into her e-mails with pedantic pleasure over the many weeks she'd traveled around England. Her sudden return to the American turn of phrase before her e-mails had abruptly stopped was another symptom something was seriously wrong. Historically, Joan assumed a persona, whether British or Native American, and carried it to the bitter end.

Rose forced herself from thoughts of Joan, watching the men fling their sharp metal darts at the target.

Drummond's gardener was a wildly indifferent player, tossing his darts without pause, either missing the target completely or hitting almost dead center.

Rose found herself unable to drag her attention from the knot of men. The hostile gardener had a long, lean body that appealed to her even if the grubby exterior wrappings did not.

He made a spectacularly bad throw, hitting a sign that read, "Women of Easy Virtue Welcome." His cronies burst into jeers.

"Vic. You're a royal pain in the ass. Can't you do any better?" one dart player called out.

"Yeah, Drummond. You're a bloody shame," the bartender said, but without any real heat.

Drummond.

Rose's head began to pound. She jumped to her feet, then froze. What was she going to do? Challenge the man in front of his friends?

A young woman brought Rose's steak and kidney pie over to the table. As the barmaid set out the silverware and a napkin, Rose subsided to her seat. "Is the guy with the Sting shirt the novelist V. F. Drummond?"

"He is."

The woman had a soft English complexion and fair blonde hair tied up with a pink bow the color of her cheeks.

She also sported so many silver rings in her eyebrows, nose, and the center of her lower lip, she glittered.

"Could you introduce me to him?" Rose asked.

"Barman won't like it if you bother him," the waitress said. "Here he's entitled to his privacy. He's just one of us."

"Thank you anyway," Rose said. The barmaid nodded and returned to her place behind the bar. Light flirting by the dart players told Rose the woman was Nell, wife of Will the bartender, who could be her twin, minus the face metal.

Nell's husband looked like a work-out king, and Rose imagined if anyone bothered V. F. Drummond, Will would set him straight.

Rose chewed her lip and watched the dart game. The good-natured ribbing the author took for his erratic play showed he was a regular in the pub.

She toyed with her pie, poking at a lump of meat and trying to decide whether it was steak or kidney, though she thought whatever it was would come back up her throat if it passed her lips. She rehearsed several opening statements she could make to Mr. V. F. Who-the-hell-did-he-think-he-was-Drummond.

Finally, she thrust her spoon into the thick crust on the pie and went to the bar. The dart players eyed her. No one gave an inch when she planted herself in front of the author.

"Mr. Drummond? I believe I asked you a question this afternoon. You haven't given me an answer yet."

Drummond, who was propped on his elbows, stared at her in the mirror behind the bar. He drained his glass and turned around, though he kept one elbow on the edge of the bar. "I sent it by e-mail."

"You'll have to tell me what the message said because I don't have a computer." She clenched her teeth together to hold back other words—tart words of frustration.

"Why don't you wait till you get back to Prince of Prussia, or wherever, and read it then. It'll still be there."

"You know something, Mr. Drummond—"

"Vic. I prefer Vic."

"Thank you, but I prefer *Mr.* Drummond. You could have

told me who you were. I'm not a stalker. I asked you a simple question. Common courtesy—"

He straightened up and frowned. "Common courtesy, *Ms*. Early, suggests you don't just walk into someone's garden and start asking him personal questions."

The bartender and the other dart players drew a step or two closer to their friend.

Whether surrounded by friends, or standing alone, Drummond was far more daunting than he'd been in the sunny English garden.

Rose held her place. "I knocked on the door, but no one answered."

"That was your answer." He turned his back, signaled the bartender, and pointed to his empty glass.

"I suppose because you're famous, you think you can be as rude as you like."

"Miss." Nell hooked Rose's arm. "Finish your pie and go."

Rose let the woman tug her away. She sat down and took up her spoon, but her hand shook so much, she dropped it, splattering gravy across her sleeve.

"Shit," she muttered, dabbing at the stains with her napkin. Her eyes welled with tears. She fought them, concentrating on the spill.

Vic Drummond half sat, half fell, into the chair across from her. He put his glass down along with one filled with something clear and bubbly. "A little sparkling water will take that out."

She nodded and dipped her napkin into the seltzer.

"You're not going to cry over a few spots, are you?" Drummond asked. He stretched out his legs and crossed his feet at the ankles. He lit a cigarette and directed smoke-rings at the blackened beams overhead.

"I'll cry if I want to," Rose said.

He broke into the song with a credible American accent. A friend at the bar shouted for him to shut his gob.

She couldn't help smiling.

"Feeling better?" he asked.

"I'd feel much better if you'd answer my question."

"Why don't you answer one of mine first? You're from some town in Pennsylvania I've never heard of, you're obviously upset about something, and I don't think you're the usual autograph seeker. So why don't you tell me what you're doing in Marleton."

"*King* of Prussia is near Valley Forge. Surely you've heard of that place? Where Washington wintered his troops before whipping the British?"

"I'm a little vague on that part of history, though I seem to remember Washington was an abominable general. You're not here to quell the British on this side of the pond, are you?"

"No. I'm looking for my sister, Joan." Tears crowded her eyes. She would not cry in front of this man. "She's not at The Rose and Thistle. She doesn't answer e-mail or phone calls. I don't know what to do."

ROSE EARLY POKED ABOUT in her pie.

Vic considered her over the twisting smoke of his cigarette. "Did you pick the B-and-B because of the name?" he asked.

She shook her head. "Joan picked it. She said it summed up our relationship. We're always at odds with each other. Now . . . I don't know where she's gone."

"Probably to the coast to lie in the sun."

Rose shook her head. "She left some things behind. Important things."

Vic stubbed out his smoke and watched Rose make mush of her pie. Except for her accent, she could have been an Irish colleen with her freckled complexion and reddish-brown hair. Although he wasn't sure the red was genuine.

Her jeans and shirt were all-American, though. The designer name was stitched on the front pocket of her top, a white, long-sleeved jumper with brown splotches on the sleeve. And a few spots on her lovely, all-American chest, though he doubted she knew that.

He signaled for another pint. "So your sister left a few

things behind. I'm always nipping around to the shops for things I've forgotten to pack."

"I'm not talking toothpaste or razors. She left a camera lens, some research material. Your book."

"Maybe she considered it all rubbish. I've been tossed in the dust bin before."

"Your book might be trash, but the lens isn't. And she wouldn't abandon her research materials before she'd finished her book."

"She was a writer?"

"*Is.* Is a photojournalist. A pretty famous one, too. Her last book was on Pueblo pottery."

"Marleton's pretty far from the pueblo, Ms. Early."

"Rose. I know, but that's Joan." She leaned forward. Her intensity came at him in almost tangible waves. "This latest book is on church art. It doesn't matter what the subject is, if Joan considers it worthy of a book, she puts her heart into it. I don't care if she was going to the shore or dining with the queen, she'd no more leave her research material behind than her camera lens."

She dug in the rucksack by her feet. She set a chunky black object on the table. "It's just like one I have at home. Dad gave us our first serious camera when we turned twelve. I still have mine and all the lenses, and I know Joan still has hers. She'd never part with this one."

Vic picked up the lens. He noticed the garden dirt still beneath his nails, and felt a flush of embarrassment rise on his cheeks. He was suddenly intensely aware that he'd been letting himself go since his aunt's death, hadn't had his hair cut in weeks—or shaved for two days, either.

Rose tapped the initials. "Joan marks everything. That's why I know it's hers."

He shrugged. "So she left a few bits behind. Maybe she intends to come back for them after she goes . . . somewhere."

"Look. I've asked myself these same questions. She didn't just leave the stuff behind. She boxed it up and put it in the bottom of a broom closet. Way in the back."

"Then I fancy she'll be back for it."

"It doesn't make sense. She paid for the month of July, packed everything but the box, stopped answering my phone calls, and drove off." Rose toyed with her pie. "I might agree she just wanted to get away if it weren't for her e-mail messages."

Vic eyed the mishmash Rose had made of her supper. His stomach growled a protest of too much beer and too little food. He called out to Nell to bring him an order of fish and chips.

"What about her e-mail?" he asked. Vic didn't know why he was questioning Rose Early. His natural need to snoop, his Aunt Alice would have said.

"Joan's e-mails were becoming very . . . weird is the only word I can think of. Then they stopped. The same day she left the Rose and Thistle."

Nell set two fish and chip orders in front of them. "Thought you might find this more to your liking, miss," Nell said and swept away Rose's spurned steak and kidney pie.

"How'd she e-mail you if you can't?"

Rose stared at him, her grayish-green eyes wide. "Good point. I didn't think of that. How *did* she e-mail me?"

He doused his chips with vinegar. "I think you should visit the library. They have at least a dozen computers. If your sister used them, Mary Garner will remember her."

"I'll go now."

Before Rose could leap from her seat, he put a hand on her arm. "The library is closed at this hour." He watched Rose's face shift from optimistic to disappointed to blank.

She sat back into her seat. She picked at her fish and chips, and he suspected her thoughts were far from the pub.

When he'd finished his supper, he leaned on his elbows and lit his last cigarette.

She set her fork beside her barely touched plate and leaned her elbows on the table in imitation of him.

"So, Mr. Drummond. You haven't answered my question. Do you believe in evil?"

4

MRS. BENNETT GREETED FATHER Nigel as she unfolded her stool in front of the Marleton tapestry. She opened her sewing box and hummed as she selected a length of wool. The light was dim in this part of the church, but she didn't mind. Her eyes were still sharp and the spotlights that shone on the nave altar were strong enough for her work.

"How long will you be here?" Father Nigel asked. "I've papers to run over to Stratford, and I'm not sure when Father Donald will be back."

"Then just leave me the key," Mrs. Bennett said. "There's a moth hole will take a bit of time. I'll lock everything up right and tight for you."

Father Nigel, a fleshy man of fifty-five, dug in his trouser pocket and drew out a shiny key. "Don't forget. We must all be more vigilant since those thugs broke into the shop."

"I don't know what's gotten into children these days. Stealing from a church gift shop! Did they do much damage?"

"Enough, Mrs. Bennett. They broke the cash register though it was empty. Took the crosses and some little gold bookmarks." Father Nigel shrugged. "I'm glad the church plate is in a proper safe. What a disaster that would have been had any of that gone missing."

"The police will catch them."

The priest shook his head. "That's what Father Donald says, but I've my doubts. Now, I've got to take this report to the bishop."

"In Stratford, you said?"

"At the symposium on youth crime. Unfortunately, the bishop will use our break-in as more proof youth programs should be nothing but sports, or arts and crafts."

Mrs. Bennett smiled up at Father Nigel. "We know different, don't we?"

He smiled back. "Indeed. We know what's best for them, you and I."

She threaded her needle while the vicar walked down the long nave of the church and out the front door.

The gift shop was closed, the tourists filling their bellies in the pubs and tea shop. This was the hour Mrs. Bennett liked best, when she had the medieval church and the tapestry all to herself. Well, almost to herself she thought when she heard the scratching of creatures overhead.

It was her greatest work, the care and maintenance of the Marleton tapestry, and she skimmed her fingers along the lustrous surface of the panel. It depicted the armies of crusaders who had rallied to fight for God in Jerusalem.

As her needle flew, she let her mind wander to Vic Drummond. He'd been practically an orphan when his aunt, Alice Drummond, had taken him in. What with his father fornicating in London and his mother on chemotherapy, there'd been little choice for the lad. Now Alice was dead. Bless her little black heart.

Mrs. Bennett glanced along the tapestry and frowned. Scooting her stool down a few yards, she began to work on a crusader. He was just one of the masses of men amid the horses and foot soldiers marching off to war. Ill-patched he was by a mediocre seamstress in the early part of the century, but he would be lovely when she finished him. Quite perfect, in fact.

And as to moth holes, there wasn't one to be found. They wouldn't dare.

VIC DRUMMOND SAT IN front of his laptop. It was midnight. He cracked his knuckles and broke open another pack of cigarettes.

Did he believe in evil?

He'd lied when he'd said no in his e-mail to Rose Early. He'd only laughed and left her when she'd asked again.

He was paid handsomely to tell stories with evil as the lynch-pin to the plots.

How could he not believe?

His aunt, dead now for seven weeks, had a copy of each of his books. He pulled *Do You Believe in Evil?* from a shelf and flipped through it.

He had signed Joan Early's copy of the book, though Rose had not mentioned that fact. He'd agreed to autograph Joan's book because of the dog-eared pages and notes in the margins. Writing in a book was a reprehensible habit according to his aunt, and he practiced it himself with guilty pleasure.

Joan Early's notes had fascinated him as they echoed questions he'd pondered when first sketching out his plot.

Could only inanimate objects absorb evil? What about pets? Could objects pass their evil on if they didn't make direct contact from one source to another?

She'd also found two minor factual errors in the book to his slight embarrassment.

"Bugger this." He slammed the book and shoved it back onto the crowded shelf.

He sat at the laptop and began to write. His story poured from his fingertips, dredged up from the bog of his brain until three o'clock in the morning when he became aware his back and fingers ached.

The laptop screen glared in the dark sitting room. Some-where outside, a dog barked.

Vic skimmed over the last few lines he'd written. A cold chill filled him; sweat broke on his hands. He rubbed them on his thighs and then used the touch pad to scroll back a page.

The priests gathered in the small sitting room and gazed on the corpse in its fine wooden coffin, placed where the old couch used to be.

Shafts of moonlight poured through the windows and pooled around the coffin. The corpse was naked, skin yellow in comparison to its soft bed of white satin and lace.

A stench of decay hung in the air.

Church bells tolled the hour—twelve thuds that sounded like muffled heartbeats.

A woman shoved between the priests and clutched the edge of the coffin. "Vic. Wake up. Wake up. It's me, Aunt Alice. Can't you hear me?"

The corpse opened its eyes. The woman held her hand over the body. On her palm lay a packet of cigarettes.

"Smoking is a dirty habit," she said.

She dropped the packet onto the corpse's chest. The packet shimmered in the moonlight, then shifted and moved.

Within the shadows of the crumpled packet appeared a pair of small red embers.

Then they blinked.

Something . . . a fingernail? . . . A claw? . . . darted out and scratched the corpse on its bare chest. A line of blood welled. The corpse opened his eyes. His mouth worked, then formed a silent scream.

Gooseflesh broke like old lizard skin on the naked body.

"Vic," the old woman whispered.

She stood tall and thin in a blue silk suit, her eyes as red as those in the packet, as red as burning coals in a

death-pale face. Her fingers, now rotting at the finger-
tips, pointed at the cigarette pack.
"They will kill you. They killed me."

Vic rubbed a bead of sweat from his brow as it crawled
down his temple. He selected the text, text he couldn't remember writing, text that had nothing to do with the ring of
a murderer, and hit the delete key.

He needed a smoke, but when he put out his hand, the
desktop was empty. He glanced around. On the floor beside
the couch lay a crumpled packet of cigarettes. The last time
he'd noticed them, they'd been next to his laptop.

5

ROSE PULLED ON HER backpack and struck off for the village on her second day in Marleton. The rising sun shone through the mist that wreathed the trunks of the pear trees. The fields beyond looked insubstantial, like a set in a Shakespearean play.

The grassy verge of High Street was starred with the tiny daisies and touched with dew. Edgar's Tea Shop sported a striped pink canopy, three wrought-iron tables outside, and a white-board that announced breakfast was being served.

A Miss Marple type in brogues and unseasonable tweeds occupied one of the tables. She did not look up as Rose sat at the next table, her attention riveted to her newspaper, a tabloid with a lurid headline about Satan worshipers loose in the Scottish highlands.

A Valkyrie of a woman with a pink-striped apron rushed out of the shop to take Rose's order.

"Would you like a proper English breakfast, then, Miss?" the woman, who introduced herself as Mrs. Edgar, asked.

"Oh." Rose, a plain bagel and black coffee kind of person, quailed at the thought of what a full English breakfast might include.

"Of course you do," Mrs. Edgar said and turned away.

"She'll have something else, she will," the elderly patron said, lifting her gaze from her paper.

"And what business is it of yours, Mrs. Watkins?" Mrs. Edgar asked. She flicked her apron hem at a fly that buzzed near an open pot of jam on the elderly woman's table.

Rose wondered if this was the mother of her own Mr. Watkins, though she saw no family resemblance between the two.

"It should be everyone's business—a person's health."

"Ah—" Rose began but fell silent when Mrs. Edgar speared her with a sharp glare.

"I know what young people want, and it isn't a load of greasy—" Mrs. Watkins said.

"Grease! There's no grease here." Mrs. Edgar's ample bosom quivered with indignation.

Rose dove into the moment of silence. "I'll have that full breakfast. And some scones with cream and jam, as well, thank you."

"See." Mrs. Edgar swept into the shop with her nose in the air.

Mrs. Watkins snapped her paper and held it before her face, giving Rose a respite from her pointed disapproval.

Rose opened her backpack and pulled out the journal where she kept business expenses and notes. As she paged through her calendar, she felt a pang of conscience. She'd forgotten to cancel a family portrait session. The Parkers booked every summer for a Christmas portrait. There were few years that they did not add a new grandchild or pet to the gathering. She flipped her cell phone open, punched a few keys, then realized that while Joan might have a phone with global access, she did not.

"The curse of a civilized society," said a voice.

She looked up and smiled. V. F. Drummond cleaned up rather nicely. He still looked unmowed, but he'd shaved. His jeans were clean though his over-sized sweater had a hole near the shoulder.

"My phone?" she asked.

He sat down and yawned. "Ruin everyone's privacy. Think the damned things should be banned." He pulled a pack of cigarettes from his pocket.

"I'll have none of that, Vic Drummond," Mrs. Edgar said. She set a huge, linen-draped tray on the table, complete with two cups. She tucked the receipt under a saucer with one hand and plucked the cigarettes from Drummond's hand with the other.

Rose suppressed a smile. Mrs. Edgar stalked off with a glare in the direction of the paper-perusing Mrs. Watkins.

"May I?" Drummond asked, although he did not wait to pour himself a cup of very dark tea. "Best breakfast in Marleton." He gestured with his cup to her plate.

It held eggs, sautéed mushrooms, bacon, and stewed tomatoes. A silver toast rack, a basket of scones, and a pot of clotted cream surrounded the plate. A jar of jam—homemade by the look of it—jostled for space with another of marmalade. Rose slathered the marmalade on the toast.

"No butter?" Drummond asked, plucking the toast from her fingertips and consuming it in three bites.

"Butter would be overdoing it, I think." She snatched the scones out of his reach. "If you're hungry, order your own breakfast."

"Why, when I can have yours?"

He leaned on his elbows and smiled.

Rose kept her hand on the rack, and fought the attraction of his infectious grin. Something told her the smile sprang from habit, not spontaneity.

"You won't keep your figure long if you eat that lot, anyway." He gestured to the plate with her fork.

Admitting defeat, she surrendered the greater portion of her breakfast to him.

"So, when do I get an answer to my question?" She picked at her scone.

"Who were you trying to ring?" he evaded, mopping up egg with her toast.

"My studio. I left in such a hurry, I forgot to arrange another photographer for one of my shoots."

"I can help you out with that call." He poured tea into her cup and topped off his own.

Rose lifted the delicate cup to her lips and forced herself to take a sip. Tea was meant to be cold. Served over ice with thick wedges of lemon. "How?"

He wagged his eyebrows. "Come on over to my place."

The lady beside them shot to her feet with a deep sigh. She struck off down High Street, her back rigidly straight, her body vibrating with disapproval.

Rose kept her attention on the author. She couldn't decide if his flirtatious manner was genuine or false. "I think I'll just find the nearest pay phone," she said.

"Telephone box. It's a telephone box here." He nodded across the street at the Pig and Pie.

To her disappointment, she did not see the expected red wood and glass structure, but a plastic booth with advertisements on it.

"How one's myths are shattered," she said.

She shifted her backpack onto her shoulder and dug some bills from her pocket. He placed a hand over hers when she put the money on the tray.

"I'll take care of the bill. After all, I ate most of it."

His hand was warm. And very clean. He did not remove it and she didn't try to pull her fingers away.

He curled her fingers around the money.

"That won't quite cover it anyway. Expensive is Mrs. Edgar's." He slid the bill from under the linen napkin and tucked it into his pocket.

He squeezed her hand. "Now let me treat you to that phone call, too."

Rose knew Joan would find a man like V. F. Drummond appealing. They'd probably screw their brains out for a few weeks then go their separate ways without a backward glance or a single regret. Rose wasn't made that way. She'd survived a disastrous marriage and a few subsequent, lackluster affairs. None of them had been easy to fall into or out of.

She withdrew her hand. "Thanks, but what I really need is a better phone."

"Whatever you desire, we have it." He put his hands on her shoulders and twirled her toward the village center. Shops stood shoulder to shoulder, some with mullioned windows, all with facades in varied shades of the rich honey-colored Cotswold stone.

The author's words and touch sent a flash of confusion and heat through her body. She slid from under his grasp and headed for the British Telecom sign three shops away.

To her dismay, Drummond tagged along. British Telecom's ancient storefront belied its thoroughly modern interior. The clerk dazzled her with an array of rental phones and accessories.

Drummond draped himself over the counter and watched her a bit like a hawk watches a small bunny it's going to snatch from a patch of clover.

She selected a phone and cringed at the cost of the short-term agreement.

Outside, while Drummond rocked on his heels, hands in pockets, she called Joan, got her voice mail, and left the new cell phone number. Next she dialed her studio and listened to the familiar message before she was urged by the voice of her partner, Max, to leave a message.

"Max? I forgot about the Parkers," she said to the machine. "I know you'll take care of them for me. Or reschedule if you think it's best. Here's my new number." She rattled off the number of the rented phone, aware of Drummond by her shoulder. She shifted around and lowered her voice. "But don't call and bug me to come home. I'm staying until I find Joan. So, bye . . . and sorry about the Parkers."

She slotted the phone into a pocket on the outside of her backpack and said to Drummond, "Don't you have work to do?"

"When it suits me, yeah. In here." He took hold of her upper arm and steered her into a shop with newspapers and magazines. He bought a pack of cigarettes.

"How do I get rid of you?" she asked.

"Oh, you don't. You need me."

"I need to find my sister. And I want an answer to my question."

"This is the best place to look for your sister. The Marleton Library."

Drummond pointed to a glass and concrete building across from the news agent. It was a garish mistake in the street of centuries-old buildings.

He held the door and bowed Rose in with a very old-fashioned gesture. Then he bounded by her and swept a woman into his arms.

"Get away with you," the woman said with a laugh as he set her down. "What are you doing out at the crack of day? Don't you usually lie abed until the vampire hour?"

The woman looked like an older version of the late Princess Diana from her coiffed hair to her very elegant gray suit and pearls.

"Mary Garner," Drummond offered to Rose. To the librarian he said, "My American mate, here, and I want to know if Joan Early used your computers."

"Joan?" The librarian swung around and considered Rose. "I know Joan."

"When did you last see her?" Rose tried to contain her excitement. Finally, someone with an answer.

"Well now." The librarian frowned. "I can't really say. Maybe not for a few days."

"How many?" Vic Drummond asked.

"Perhaps six or seven. I saw her Friday last. That was, let me see, the twenty-fourth of June, I believe."

Rose's body went cold. Her backpack slipped off her shoulder. It hit the floor with a thud. Vic took a firm hold of her arm. "You're sure of the day, Mary?" he asked.

The woman nodded. "Yes. I was with Jack Carey at the Bell—"

Drummond interrupted her. "Have you seen Joan anywhere else around the village since Friday, then?" he asked.

Resignation that this was just another dead-end made Rose sigh.

"No. No, I'm sorry. Is something wrong?" Mary asked.

"It seems Joan's gone off without letting anyone know her destination," he said lightly.

Vic steered Rose away from the front desk. "Mary Garner's no gossip, but why give out all the bloody details?" he said by her ear.

Behind them, Mary Garner gasped. She darted past them, across an acre of burgundy carpet, and snatched a magazine from a man. He snarled like a wild thing and made a grab for the glossy periodical. It was Harry Watkins.

Vic was beside the pair in a two strides. "What's wrong?"

Harry Watkins, the proprietor of the Rose and Thistle, made a guttural sound in his throat. "We don't need this filth in our library."

"If you don't like it, don't read it," Mary said.

Rose looked at the magazine Watkins had torn in two. It was an American fashion magazine.

"Tells how to suck a man's cock, it does," Watkins said.

"Lower your voice." Mary glanced about, but the library was almost deserted.

"Why? If a thing's decent we can shout about it at the top of our lungs." Watkins shook a quivering finger at the magazine cover.

Next to a photograph of a popular movie star in a clingy red dress, the magazine cover said, "Ten Ways to Please Him in Bed."

"*That* magazine is very popular with the younger crowd. Unlike you, they make contributions to the book fund. You're going to pay for that magazine." Mary's voice trembled.

Vic scooped up the offending magazine and put out his arms. He herded both of them toward the desk. "If I remember correctly, this matter was debated at budget meeting. Bring it up again if you're not happy with—"

"And you!" Watkins interrupted in a harsh, raspy whisper. "You're no better. Filth is what you write. Utter, obscene filth. Corpses fornicating. Evil rings corrupting innocent priests. You should be banned."

"Thanks for reading." He picked up Rose's backpack and took her arm. "Come on, let's get a cup of tea."

Outside, Rose drew her arm from his grip. "Is it safe to leave them alone?"

"Mary can hold her own with that one. Harry'll try to barter American fashion rubbish for American gun rubbish. Mary will counter with a dry literary periodical. They'll compromise and buy them all—and some local rich chap will foot the bill."

"I'll take my bag, please." She held out her hand. "I need to find my sister." She swept a hand out to encompass the street. "Someone must know her besides Mary."

Vic pursed his lips and pretended to think. How could he delay her? She wore only one ring, a silver band, but she wore it on her right thumb. Not a wedding ring, then. Her skin was pale, her freckles like scattered gold dust on white silk.

He took a grip of a budding lust.

"Just because your sister hasn't returned a few e-mails doesn't mean she's missing. Maybe she met the man of her dreams."

"Don't." She shook her head. Her cinnamon hair, caught up in a plastic clip, bobbed with her denial. "Don't patronize me. I didn't fly over here because my sister failed to keep me informed of her social plans."

"Sorry, mate." He felt a compulsive desire to touch her. She gave off something intangible that made it hard to keep his hands off. She had been his first thought when hunger had struck at dawn. And it hadn't been an English breakfast kind of hunger at that.

"Don't do it again," she said. "Now, good-bye."

"We were going to have tea."

"You can have tea. I want a cup of coffee. Black. Stand-your-hair-on-end black."

Her bum looked great as she stalked away.

"I have a coffee pot," he called.

Rose wheeled around. Her eyes were bright. Shit. If she

started to cry, he'd really be in trouble. She took a deep breath and looked across the village street at the library. When she looked back, the tears were under control.

"Mr. Drummond. If you can make a cup of coffee as well as you write about fornicating corpses, I'll follow you anywhere."

6

ROSE WANDERED AROUND VIC Drummond's sitting room. It was a mix of years of love and care by Alice Drummond and a few months habitation by a man who didn't care if the dust lay on the furniture thick enough to autograph.

Alice Drummond had collected books and antiques with equal passion. The only modern convenience in the room was a laptop on a carved rosewood desk. The laptop reminded her of e-mail.

"Excuse me," she called. "Forget the coffee, I have to get back to the library. With all the brouhaha, I didn't check my e-mail. What if Joan left me a message?"

Vic appeared in a small archway between the sitting room and the kitchen. "I'll put you on my laptop as soon as I figure this out." He held up a European-style plunger coffee pot.

"So you lied." She took it from his hand and headed into the tiny kitchen.

"I didn't lie. I said I had a coffee pot."

Rose shook her head.

"I thought I'd give it a go if it would lure you to my lair." He wagged his eyebrows just as a kettle began to sing.

Rose had difficulty dredging up regret for following him home. For the first time in Marleton, she found herself relaxing in the cozy comfort of the cottage.

The kitchen windowsills overflowed with African violets—dying African violets. She measured the coffee into the pot and poured in the boiling water. After she pressed the plunger, she used a small pitcher to water the flowers.

Vic left her with a grin. She heard him tapping keys on his computer. She wanted to join him, but didn't want to appear too anxious, so she contented herself with plucking dead leaves from the plants and peering around the doorway.

"Come through," he said, offering the desk chair like a waiter in a fine restaurant.

She swallowed. What if she was making a fool of herself and Joan was lying on a beach somewhere, or had gone off with some guy? It would be more embarrassment than Rose could stand if there was a message from Joan regaling the details of her latest bedroom conquest.

"Don't be such a coward," she muttered and logged onto the Internet. She hastily skimmed her mail.

Three messages from Max. Jokes. One from a cousin in Oregon, another joke. The usual fifteen offering to enlarge her penis or refinance her mortgage and one from filthyrich@dybie.com.

She deleted the spam, logged off, and went back to the kitchen. She tested the coffee to cover her disappointment.

"Do you take anything in your coffee?" she asked when she could trust her voice to sound normal.

"Lots of cream." He opened a carton and wrinkled his nose, set it aside for another. "Or milk if I've let the cream go off."

She stood in the tiny kitchen, dominated by a large white stove and Vic Drummond. He propped himself against the door to Alice Drummond's fantastic garden.

"Nothing from your errant Joan, I suppose?" he asked.

Rose shook her head and sipped the coffee. "And nothing from you either, liar."

He presented her with an innocent look. "I swear. I answered you."

"Forget it. I don't care anymore." But Rose knew it was she who was lying. If Joan had taken the time to write in Drummond's book, make notes, scrawl her belief in evil on the final page, it did matter. But Rose wasn't going to look like a fool to this man.

The coffee was just how she liked it, strong and gritty. "Don't you have a housekeeper?"

"Or a cook?" He smiled.

His smile lifted her spirits for ten seconds, the time it took her to realize he was probably toying with her.

"I have all the trappings in London. Here," he looked around. "I like to keep things as my auntie did. Didn't like change, did Alice."

"I understand she recently passed away. I'm sorry."

He turned to look out at the garden. "She loved this place."

"What did your aunt do for a living?"

"Gardened. Helped at the library."

"A lady of leisure."

"She earned it. Alice worked in the church gift shop when I first came here to live with her. She also did whatever needed doing—repaired vestments, polished silver; served the church for twenty years." He nodded in the direction of the hulking edifice that dominated the skyline behind his aunt's small garden.

He grinned over his mug. "I used to sneak about when I was a lad and pinch a few quid from the safe when she left it open."

"What a bad boy you were." Rose wondered if it was a piece of clever fiction for entertaining tourists.

"A right devil if you asked Alice." He looked away as he said it. "They found her in the garden."

Rose went to one of the multi-paned windows draped with simple white curtains on the inside and climbing ivy on the outside. The morning sun painted the elaborate garden in a palette of pastels and soft greens. Calendar material.

For a moment she thought about the shades of color, the camera settings needed to bring out the mistiness that gathered at the bottom of the garden where a wooden gate broke a high stone wall.

"You're letting the roses get leggy," she said.

He moved next to her. "You know roses, Rosie?" He tugged a strand of her hair.

"No. The bartender at the King's Head Pub. And he knows you." She shifted from his side and poured herself more sludge from the pot.

"Sampling the local beer?" He crossed his arms and went back to leaning on the woodwork.

Her hormones bubbled. He'd pushed up the sleeves of his sweater. His arms were long and tanned, well-muscled—not the skinny ones of a man who did nothing more energetic than tap a few computer keys.

Rose concentrated on her coffee. "The beer was fine, but I was asking about Joan. And you."

"You must be very close to your sister to come all this way."

"Not so close, but I came anyway." She set her mug on a table bleached to a soft gray by years of scrubbing. "I have to go. Thanks for the coffee."

He didn't detain her, but followed her to the bright blue door.

"You've piqued my curiosity, so I hope you'll visit again and let me know how you're getting on."

"I will." She held out her hand. "Thank you for the coffee. It really was obnoxious of me to just barge into your life."

"Barge any time." He shook her hand. "And if I'm not here, you can always find me down the pub."

She resisted the impulse to ask him again if he believed in evil . . . and resisted another impulse that zinged up her arm and made her want to cling a moment longer to his warm hand.

* * *

ALL SAINTS CHURCH DOMINATED the village. Unlike the soft honey tones of the cottages and shops, the church was built of a dark, rough stone. Its ponderous shape betrayed its Norman origins. The six doors were twice her height, carved in a dark wood and strapped with iron hinges as big as her arm.

The church was cool and dim inside. Damp stone, old hymnals, and stale incense crafted a potpourri of odors in the nave.

A sign directed her to the gift shop which she found tucked just inside the front doors. The shop was crowded with tourists. She browsed the spinning racks of postcards and selected an atmospheric view of the church for Max. For her mother, lost in an Alzheimer haze in a King of Prussia nursing facility, she chose a card that showed a cottage, much like Vic Drummond's, its garden filled with bright roses.

A frowning woman, Fiona Sayer by her name tag, ruled the area behind the cash register. She called out to the shop in general that a tour group was queuing up in the nave, and they should get a move on or they'd be late.

Impulsively, Rose joined the tourists being shepherded along by a tall man who might have been Sean Connery's younger brother.

She followed the group to a set of spiral steps that led to the bell tower. Halfway up, she knew the decision was a mistake. The narrow, enclosed space brought on a wave of dizziness.

Escape was impossible. A dozen tourists clogged the stairs above, a large Swedish family hemmed her in from below.

As she waited what seemed an interminable time on the claustrophobic stairs, she closed her eyes and imagined herself at the New Jersey shore. She stood with feet in the surf, eyes on the horizon, nothing but blocks of shoreline to the left and right.

She heard the shuffle of sandals. A whisper of voices. Chanting.

When Rose opened her eyes, the sounds disappeared. Carried on the tide, she made it to the top step without vomiting. Fresh air washed the cobwebs from her head.

To Rose's disappointment, no bells hung in the room where they exited from the tower stairs. Pairs of ropes hung in the ringing chamber, hooked high out of reach, the only indication that overhead was a belfry filled with eight massive bells weighing tons. Plaques on the wall honored past ringers who'd excelled at the art in past years.

"Sadly, the bells no longer ring at All Saints," Sean Connery's brother said. "We've not had a company of ringers in more than twelve years. The bells aren't always silent, however. We're sometimes honored with visiting members of the Royal Bell Ringers."

The guide indicated another windy set of steps for those who wished to view the belfry.

Facing another shoulder-wide set of steps or sitting with the less fit on what looked like rolled-up party tents, she opted for pacing the airy chamber.

She peeked into an open doorway. As her eyes adjusted to the gloom, she realized it was an attic extending the length of the nave, spanned by a long catwalk. The vaulted ceiling of the nave beneath the catwalk looked like a snow-covered mountain, curving out to the church walls.

"Ah, miss." The guide tapped her shoulder. "You can't stay here."

"May I take a quick picture?" She pointed into the attic space.

"Can't do any harm," the man said. He pushed the door open. Rose stepped up onto the catwalk. It was surprisingly sturdy. She gripped the iron railings and walked a few feet out over the nave's ceiling. Fresh air stirred her hair from windows that pierced the walls illuminating the smooth, white-washed expanse below.

She squeezed off a few shots of the roof within a roof.

"Most of the planks on the gangway are over nine hundred years old," the guide said.

Rose took a hasty step back.

"Oh, it's perfectly safe." The guide joined her. His heavier tred shook the gangway. Some of her confidence disappeared. Her stomach did a little dance.

"See those protuberances?" the guide asked. "Can you guess what they are?

Spaced at distant intervals along the sloping nave ceiling were wooden spikes at least eight inches square. "Roof beams?" she asked.

"Close. They're the other end of the ceiling bosses. Many of those are older than these planks."

She focused on the blocky protuberances. The guide stomped the gangway. It vibrated violently. She fumbled her camera, just catching it before it tumbled to the sloping ceiling below.

"Stop, please." The camera was the latest in digital marvels, its capabilities so extensive, she'd pretty much abandoned the rest of her equipment. Replacing it would be a financial hardship.

The guide blocked her way. He grinned and licked his lips. The group burst into the ringing chamber with the babel of different languages. "Time to go," the guide said.

Rose secured her camera in her backpack before following the guide from the attic, grateful for the crowd in the sunlit room, unsure if the man had meant to scare her or tease her.

Each step down the tower stairs ratcheted her nausea up a notch. The narrow space, the smell of damp stone, filled her with a wild desire to shove past the tourists who dawdled along in front of her. They were sardines in a can. A stone can at that.

When they reached the bottom, Rose covered her mouth and headed straight for the wooden seats in the nave. She stumbled, taking out a cluster of chairs like a bowling ball knocks off pins.

"Miss?" Someone called. The guide. Rose shied from the man's touch, knocking more chairs out of alignment.

"I'm . . . dizzy."

"You're white as a ghost." The tour guide's words pinged off the stone walls and floor around her.

She moaned. Many hands pulled her to a chair and pressed her head between her knees. She closed her eyes and gulped for air. A soft indistinct whisper, a shuffle of feet on stone, sandaled feet, filled her head as it had in the stairwell.

But all the shoes that crowded her limited view from between her knees varied from wing-tip to grass-stained sneakers. Familiar grass-stained sneakers.

Vic Drummond massaged the back of her neck.

She swallowed and closed her eyes. Slowly, the waves of dizziness and nausea passed to be replaced by a throbbing precursor to a headache. When she lifted her head, the author kept his hand in place, his fingers kneading the skin under her hair.

"Look what happens when you skip breakfast," he said.

Rose shoved Drummond's hand away. "I'm fine now."

"You're still a touch white, Miss," the tour guide said. "Can I take you over to the vicarage? For some tea perhaps?"

The guide's smile did not reach his eyes.

"No, thank you." Vic Drummond helped her to her feet. "Are you stalking me?" she asked him.

"You're not that good-looking."

Without a word, she headed for the exit. Outside, one hand on the iron railing, she carefully descended the ancient marble steps. When she reached the pavement, she followed it along the south side of the church. Drummond dogged her footsteps. She sat on a bench within a huge arched gateway to the cemetary. He sat uncomfortably close to her, his thigh against hers. She shifted from his warmth. Did the man have a furnace inside?

"Why are you here?" she asked, her headache miraculously gone.

"I remembered something I wanted to ask you. And if a tourist isn't in the shops, she's here."

She pretended to ignore him. She yawned.

Not that good-looking.

Joan would second that thought. Highlight your hair. Use more makeup. Buy better clothes.

"Aren't you curious about my question?"

"What's chocolate flake?" She pointed to an ice cream truck parked in front of the church.

Before she could stop him, he'd bounded over to the cart and returned with a dish of vanilla ice cream. Jammed into the mound of ice cream was a blocky stick of crumbly chocolate. It made her think of the bosses thrust through the vaulted ceiling of the nave.

"Feeling better?" he asked.

The ice cream was cold and delicious. "I guess I was just hungry," Rose said after she'd licked her plastic spoon clean. Did jet lag and hunger cause hallucinations? "And thank you for treating me."

He shrugged. "My question?"

"Go ahead." She feigned another bored yawn.

"Why would you want to know if *I* believe in evil? What has that to do with your sister?"

Rose chased a few crumbs of chocolate around her bowl. "Joan wrote in your book—everywhere. But under the last line, you know, where the priest is asked if he believed, Joan wrote, 'I believe.' A few weeks ago . . . I don't think she'd have written those words."

He waited in silence.

"You set up the whole book around this essential question. Joan isn't superstitious or religious. The last time she was in a church—outside her work on this book, that is— was my wedding."

"Married are you?"

"Divorced. Focus, please. Reading Joan's words sent a shiver down my spine. And not knowing where she went, not being able to find anyone who knows either—not knowing what she's doing. . . ."

Sitting beside this man in the dazzling sunshine, eating ice cream, it seemed ridiculous to think anything had happened to Joan. Or believe something dire had happened because of a few words written in a horror novel.

Or that whispering ghosts in sandals existed.

Rose felt stupid. A fool. An unattractive fool.

"You still haven't told me why you want to know if I believe," he said. He took her bowl and set it on the ground. The grass here, like that at her B and B, was studded with daisies. Rose pulled out her digital camera on it and hid her confusion by adjusting the settings and shooting a few pictures of the tiny flowers.

"I wanted to know if the idea for the book had come from an inner belief of yours or if it was all just fiction," she finally said. "To convince Joan, you'd have to be incredibly persuasive. I think she was deeply influenced by your book."

Vic Drummond stood up and shoved his hands into the back pockets of his jeans. "I have a very fertile imagination. The book's fiction."

He sounded hard, the frosty gardener again. She rested the camera in her lap, casually changed settings, and shot him, a tall figure standing in the shadows of a towering church. A winged gargoyle that hid a waterspout was poised at the roof's edge as if to swoop down and snatch him up.

"So what happened in there?" he asked.

His tone softened. Making amends for his sharp tongue?

"I felt dizzy, that's all. I'm fine now."

"Did your sister make a habit of running off?"

Rose shrugged. "I wish I could say no and be sure of it, but I can't. She was a bit of a free spirit. I just had this gut feeling that I had to come over and find her."

"I believe in gut feelings," Vic said.

"Truthfully, it's more than a feeling." She broke off. She wasn't ready to admit that Joan had asked Rose to meet her in Marleton, had made the request seem urgent. Rose wasn't ready to admit she'd ignore the repeated requests, either.

VIC TOOK ROSE'S BOWL to the ice cream cart and disposed of it.

When he returned, Rose had collected herself. "Joan said there was something weird about the cathedral."

"Church." He sat on the grass near Rose's feet and looped his arms around his knees.

"Church? Sure looks like a cathedral to me."

"A cathedral is a bishop's seat. No bishop, no cathedral. We're just plain All Saints Church of Marleton."

Here and there, tourists sat as they did, enjoying the sun or shade, some eating ice cream, some with heads on rucksacks, dozing. Vic wondered what Rose had been photographing with her clever camera. He idly speculated about what Joan had shot with hers.

"Churches are weird places," he said noncommittally.

Rose nodded and raised her camera again.

He followed the line of her aim and saw only broken slate and crumbling buttresses.

"Joan was shooting in the nave and thought she saw something moving in the shadows."

Rose tucked her camera away in her bag.

"And?" he prompted.

She lifted her eyes to the church tower. "Joan thought the shadow was a gargoyle."

7

ROSE FOLLOWED VIC AROUND the perimeter of the church. He explained that the archway was a nineteenth century lytch gate, a place for the coffin and mourners to shelter from rain while awaiting the priest.

For one fleeting moment, Rose considered telling Drummond about the shuffling sandals and the low whispers where none should have been.

"Thank you for not laughing about Joan's gargoyle," she finally said, chickening out on revealing her own hallucinations. It was okay to say Joan was loony, but Rose wasn't ready to admit to anything personal.

He shrugged. "Nothing funny about it. Your sister thought she saw something she couldn't explain."

"Still, it sounds impossible."

"I'm a bit more open-minded than some."

He smiled and she thought he should be arrested for that grin. It was deadly on the composure, even to women who weren't good-looking. That thought sobered her rather quickly.

"My sister wrote a total of twelve e-mails about the incident. I'm ashamed to say I finally wrote her back and said, 'Move on, you've beaten that dead gargoyle enough,' or some such words. She never mentioned it again."

He tucked his fingers into the back pockets of his jeans. "Where was your sister when she saw the ghoulie?"

"In the nave, photographing . . . I can't remember what. What I can remember is that she said the gargoyle flitted between the shadows of some pillars carved with statues. Almost as if it had stepped down from one of them."

"Let's see if we can find the spot, shall we?" He took Rose's arm and led her to front doors.

"Mr. Drummond—"

"Please, Vic. Mr. Drummond's my father."

"Vic, then. Thank you for taking me seriously. You're the first person to really listen to me. Even Max, at home, thought I was crazy to feel this panic."

Vic pulled the huge door open and ushered her in.

A rush of musty air greeted them.

"Rosie." Vic snapped his fingers in front of her face.

"Sorry." She felt the heat on her cheeks. Unattractive and foolish. "I was thinking that my church door is maybe twenty years old, and it's in worse condition than this one. The brochure said these were installed in 1520."

Vic led her around a family of tourists to the center of the nave. Side aisles ran the length of it, separated by rows of ponderous stone pillars. Rose frowned up at them. "Anglo-Saxon?"

"Norman."

At the end of the nave stood an altar with tall iron stands holding candles at least a yard tall. Flanking the altar was a beautiful high pulpit of glossy English oak and a lesser structure made of iron, the lectern.

Vic leaned on the pulpit. "Behold the saints."

Carved figures ringed the base of two pillars that held

aloft the arched roof of the chancel. Each saint lifted his face
to heaven. Rose recognized them from several of Joan's contact sheets.

Spots poured light down upon their heads and cast
grotesque shadows, but there was nothing to see but im-
moveable stone.

To the left of the pulpit, where the north transept should
be, was a stone wall draped with a tapestry. The ghosts of
arched windows could be seen in the gloom overhead.
"What happened?"

"A fire. World War II was on, so there weren't funds to re-
place the glass. It was blocked up then. The tapestry was a
gift from a local patroness. It hides the worst of it, I suppose."

The floor tilted. Another wave of vertigo sent Rose to a
chair. "I really feel rotten."

They sat in the front row of chairs and Vic gave her a
rapid-fire dissertation on the church from the ancient altar
screen to something called reredos.

"I'd like to see the altar screen up close, if I may. Joan
took so many pictures of it."

Vic put his hand lightly on the small of her back and
guided her under a gate and past the choir stalls.

"Why the gate?" she asked.

"It's a rood screen. Back in medieval times it separated
the holy from the unwashed."

"Oh."

They waited their turn to view the altar screen. Two, thoroughly new millennium, spotlights picked up the gilding on
the carved figures.

Rose approached the altar screen with a reverence she
hadn't felt since entering the noisy, tourist-filled church.

"Designed by an artist who needed an anti-acid tablet,"
Vic said. He faked a belch to emphasize his point.

"Not much for religion are you?" she asked.

Vic shrugged. "These are the saints again. Met shabby
deaths, they did. Crucified, stoned."

Rose pulled out her camera and took a few pictures won-
dering if she could match her sister's work on these particu-

larly gruesome faces. As she did so, her stomach did a little dance. She swallowed hard and turned away in case Drummond noticed her discomfort.

"Your sister was to do a book on all this?" he asked from close behind her.

"She was commissioned by the Cotswolds Diocese. I'm a bit hazy on all the details. Joan was rather sanctimonious about her work and, and to be honest, it bored me."

As they walked away from the hot spotlights, Vic Drummond's smile took on interesting shadows. And her stomach settled in the cooler air of the nave.

Black and white, Rose thought.

I must photograph him in black and white. She turned her camera on him, unable to resist the impulse. Just as she took the photograph he bent over and rubbed away imaginary dust on the edge of the choir stall. All she had was a great shot of his ear.

"I'd think, both being photographers, you'd have an interest in each other's work," he said.

It was cool, dark, and quiet in the chancel, far from the tourists. "Joan thinks family photos, or 'kid pix' as she liked to call them, are the lowest of the low."

Rose wandered down the choir stalls. She ran her hands over the weird carvings beneath the seats and took a few shots of the distorted figures.

"Isn't this a bit macabre for a church?" she asked, pulling down a seat, and perching there with her camera on her knee.

"The misericords? No more than gargoyles."

Vic Drummond was a long, tall, alluring package. It was all she could do to keep her focus on the grotesque figures of the church seats rather than the lean lines of his body as he propped himself against a stone pillar. As a photographer, she appreciated the composition of modern man in contrast to the ancient edifice. As a woman, she appreciated the way the light angled across his face.

He stretched and made himself comfortable against the pillar. A little itch developed in her fingertip, an itch to take the shot. She raised the camera, and then lowered it just as quickly. If Joan saw photos of Drummond, she'd shriek with laughter. The thought made Rose drop the camera back into her pack.

Rose suspected Joan would make some scathing, perfectly aimed remark about Rose looking through England for her when a much more tempting quarry stood in front of her.

Rose also suspected Joan would take photos of Vic Drummond without subterfuge. And probably while he was naked . . . and after she had sucked him dry.

That image zinged heat through Rose's entire body. She dragged the clip from her hair. Her head pounded. Even the roots of her hair ached.

"I can't believe that two days ago I was in Pennsylvania minding my own business."

Vic pushed off his pillar and held out his hand. "You look like you need a cream tea at Mrs. Edgar's."

She jumped up, avoiding his hand. "Oh, I'm sorry. You're obviously hungry. Why don't you go, I'm going to . . . pray."

"What about?"

"That's an impertinent question."

"I'm not known for my manners. And we haven't found any ghoulies." He dogged her steps down the south aisle.

As infectious as his grin was, Rose could not help feeling shocked he did not gracefully drift off to his damned cream tea so she could pray.

"What are you going to pray for?" he asked.

Rose impaled him with the sternest look she could muster. "Joan."

She did her best to stalk away, not sure where she was heading, looking for a place to pray that was not peopled with milling tourists.

"You'd think a church would have somewhere to pray." He tugged her by a chapel with an iron gate—locked. They passed bays dedicated to various purposes from a seventeenth-century husband's adoration of a wife to the honoring of Marleton's war dead.

She jerked to a halt. "Here." A wooden bench she thought was called a *prie dieu* stood before the bay.

She sank to her knees. Drummond gave her a hip check, shoving her over so he could kneel with her.

"Praying for Joan, right?"

She ignored him, the warmth of his arm, and the scent of him, something earthy. *Probably rotting topiaries*, she thought uncharitably. She locked her fingers and propped her elbows on the rail

"This is uncomfortable," he said, shifting and bumping her side. "What happened to the comfy cushions?"

"They were probably stolen by Joan's gargoyle." She forced herself to think only of Joan's e-mail messages.

Suddenly, V. F. Drummond and his far-too tempting presence disappeared. She closed her eyes.

She heard a drumming, like boots on the march. The sound magnified, then softened and melted away on the draft that flirted with her hair.

Sandals—not boots. A shuffle, not a march.

"I can't pray," she said and tried to rise.

Vic Drummond settled a heavy hand on her shoulder. "So don't pray. Just meditate."

The wooden kneeler bit into her knees, but it was his hand that made meditation impossible. It was not meant to distract, just hold her in place, but it trifled with her insides. Her musings became thoughts best left at the church door.

After a few moments of uneasy silence between them, she relaxed. *These weird sensations are just hunger*. She longed for a perfectly grilled burger and maybe a milkshake, extra thick.

A languid feeling stole over her. She might liken it to those moments just before waking fully in the early morning, when she wanted to get up and start the day, but her body seemed content to remain where it was.

Her mind drifted. To last week. Last summer. Last year.

Rose tried to focus her thoughts on the plaque before her with its sobering list of names. Images of Joan intruded. Joan in all the stages of her life.

Joan. Joan. Joan.

Rose leaped to her feet and hurried down the nave. This

time, although Vic followed, he did not try to prevent her leaving.

When they reached the street that ran in front of the church, they stood on the curb waiting for a break in the slowly-crawling parade of traffic heading into the heart of the village.

"What spooked you?" he asked, but without any sarcasm in his tone. This time, he sounded as if he genuinely wanted to know.

"I couldn't get this one image out of my head." They darted between the cars and walked up the road toward the tea shop.

"My father had a prized photo in his office. It was of Joan. I've looked at that photograph for as long as I can remember and I guess that's why it suddenly popped into my head. Have you ever had a sore in your mouth? Your tongue keeps going to it?"

He nodded.

"Well, while I was trying to pray, I couldn't shake this image." She sketched the size of the photograph with her hands, estimating for him the dimensions. "I suppose at one time, it might have served as an example of my dad's work. Of how an enlargement, boldly done, oversized, could offer impact in a room. It was a black and white shot. She wore one of those frilly, Easter dresses." Rose felt a thickness in her throat. "She's clutching one of dad's cameras to her chest, the way other children clutch a beloved doll. The camera was far too large for such a small child."

"Were you jealous of her?" Vic asked.

Rose avoided Vic's gaze and the tea shop, walking past it to an arched stone bridge that crossed a broader section of the brook that wound its way out of sight and past the impossibly quaint cottages where V. F. Drummond camped.

"That's a complicated question," she finally said.

"So, give me a complicated answer."

Flower petals drifted slowly past her under the bridge. Rose pulled out her camera and caught the petals floating on the clear, rippling water.